D1744029

THE ATTIC.

A Christmas Story

Matthew Amick

MERRY CHRISTMAS

Carson's Pub.
Independent Publishing
Virginia

The first book published by Carson's Pub., Independent Publishing.

http://www.carsonspub.com

Amick, Matthew, 1975-

ISBN 0-9675024-0-3

1. United States—Fiction—Christmas—Juvenile fiction.

I. Title. 1998

Cover painting done by June Ball from a picture of Santa Claus taken during his 1982 visit of Occoquan, Virginia. The illustrations contained within this work also by June Ball of Two Sisters Gallery 302 Mill Street, Occoquan, Virginia 22125

Printed in the United States of America

First Edition

The Attic.

A Christmas Story

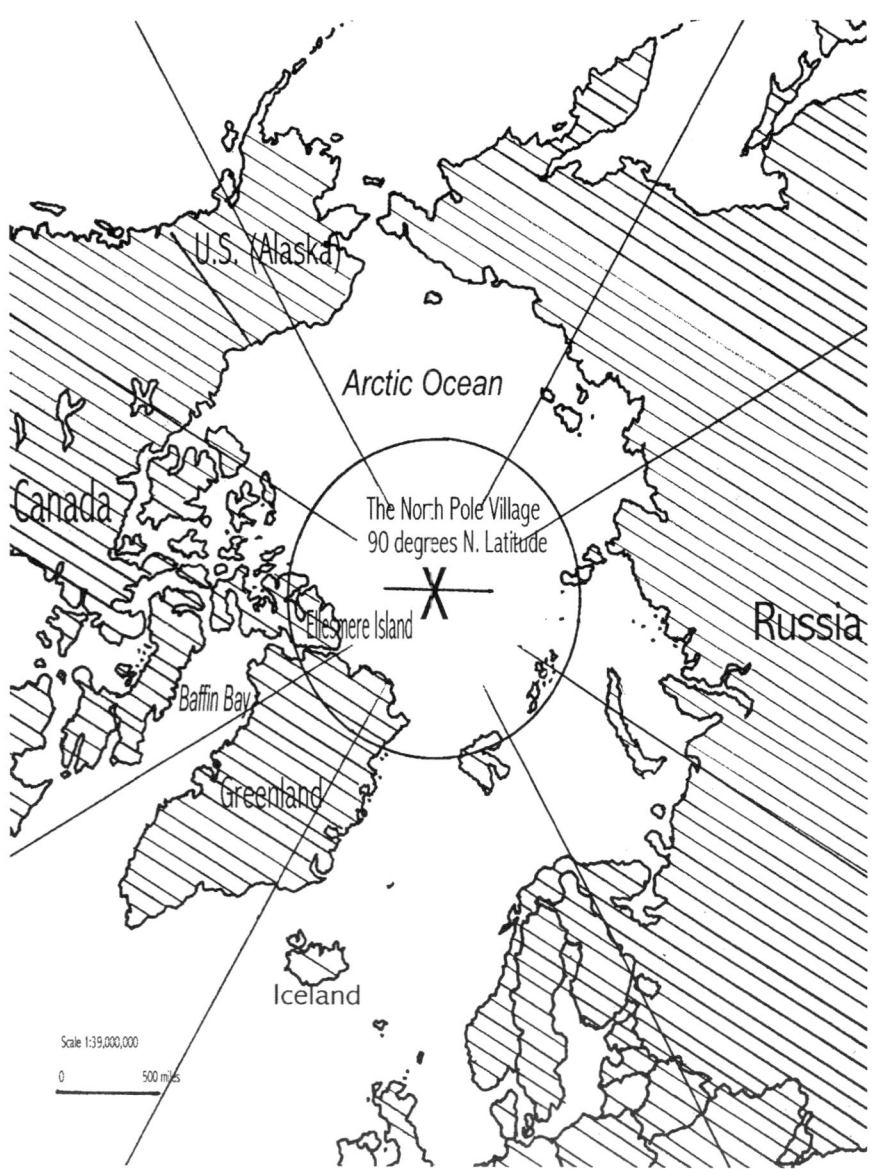

U.S. (Alaska)

Arctic Ocean

Canada

The North Pole Village
90 degrees N. Latitude
X

Ellesmere Island

Baffin Bay

Russia

Greenland

Iceland

Scale 1:39,000,000

0   500 miles

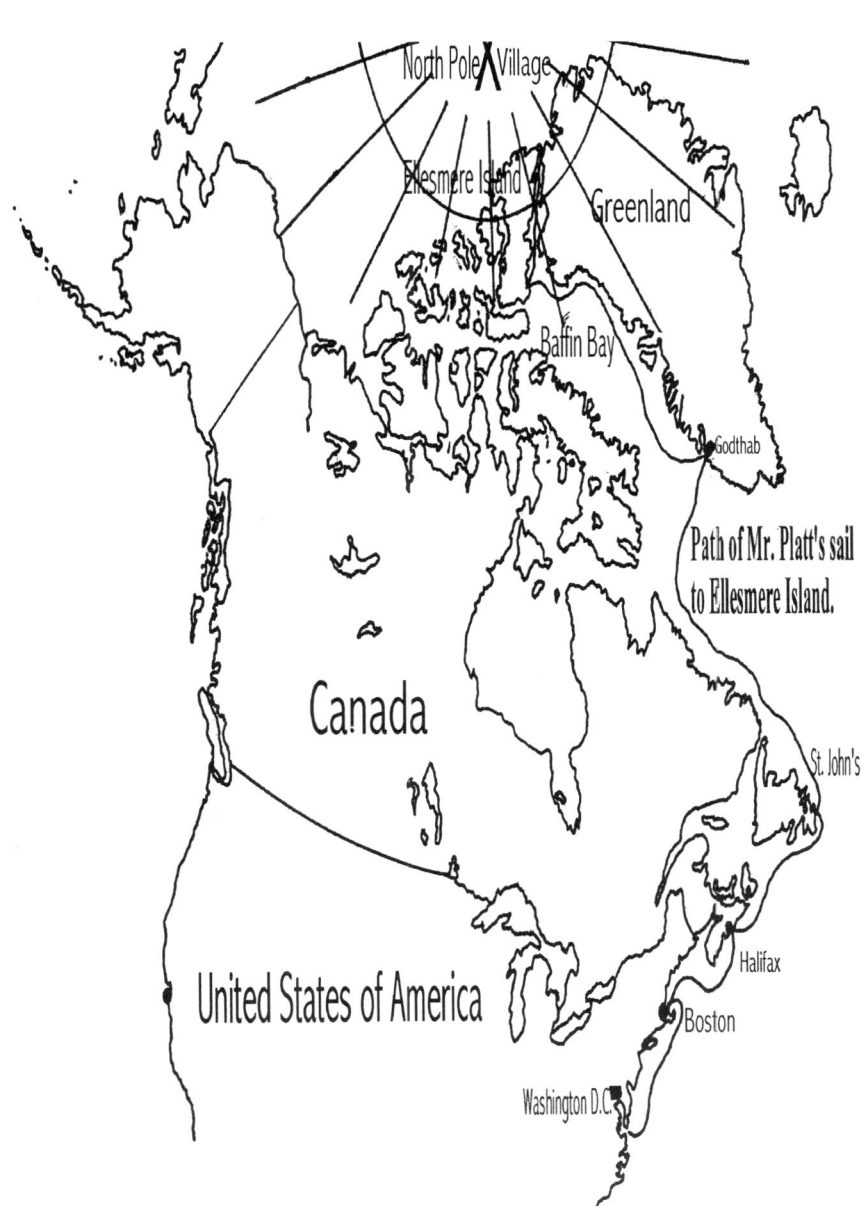

North Pole Village

Ellesmere Island

Greenland

Baffin Bay

Godthab

Path of Mr. Platt's sail
to Ellesmere Island.

Canada

St. John's

United States of America

Halifax

Boston

Washington D.C.

This book is dedicated to the Christmas spirit that makes so much wonderful possible and to two…

Brian Fairbanks
For sharing with us his contagious smile and unending passion for play

Roy H. Carson, Jr.
For giving us his image of style and humorously captivating each day

To Katie Lee and Amanda Jane

Introduction.

This book was written for one of Virginia's oldest families, the Platts, by Matthew Amick. It is based on conversations held between Mr. Amick and George Platt's Great Grandson, Ben Platt, when Ben was twenty-nine years old. The excerpts from the diary of George Platt's North Pole expedition contained in this work are taken word for word from the original.

As I sat bored in the house that my Great Grandfather built, I searched for some excitement that Christmas season of 1980. While I thought of possible activities that may pass boredom into some stage of activity, I also wanted peace from the annoyance emanating from my two younger sisters. Even though my Mother was hard at work in her kitchen, and my Dad was to open the back door on his return from work at any minute, I could no longer wait. The thick, and still thickening snow would require a large amount of suiting up if I chose to explore the great outdoors. So, I was left to the walls and their insides. Not much space was left unexplored in that house, all but my parent's room, which was off limits for whatever reason. Then, of course, there was the attic. The attic was still left untouched by these eyes, and according to my parents should stay that way. I asked myself why parents have such rules, if my attic were to suddenly become my living room and vice versa, then would I no longer be allowed in my living room? Probably. The fun places are not for children, although we may sometimes see such places if accompanied by an adult. There lies the catch of it all; what fun-loving child wishes to see such a forbidden place with an adult?

Before I venture on, allow me to fill you in on two very important facts. One, my Great Grandfather George Platt built this house long before my father was even born. I was told, and some careful excavating proved such facts, my Great Grandfather was a very sharp young man. He had a lust for exploration and knowledge, and evidently the same lust for stashing everything he ever got his hands on. So, my attic was an assortment of interesting stuff, though for as long as I can remember no one but I ever ventured up there. I assume such a venture never took place because no one was as brave as I. And partly because my Dad was told, while being raised in the same very house, that he was not to do the very thing I did. I think he still had some innate fear of the place. I guess my Great Grandfather's bravery passed over a generation. The second very important fact is this--I was a brave soul to go where I was warned not to…

BELIEVING.

As I approach the doorway that has been painted over and over at the end of the hallway I hope for the first time in my childhood career that my sisters do not quiet. Such a sudden quiet would not do much to mask my attempts at opening a sealed door at the top of a stairway not far from the kitchen where my Mom is currently laboring over a pot of venison stew (we do not tell my sisters that the stew contains deer meat, otherwise they would not eat the stuff, one of my parents strict rules of confidentiality).

I tug at the door several times in order to free it from its years of secrets, but as I begin to make my fourth and surely revealing effort, I hear the door of my Dad's truck shut. I wipe my hands on my pants and run downstairs to greet my Dad. The stagnant air that becomes a winter house is broken when Dad enters, carrying with him the evening air. Rarely does the six-foot tall, and somewhat stocky man wear a frown or even a slightly sour look when entering his house. It would be hard for him not to smile when entering a house full of wonderful smells and three adoring children. The Christmas season really makes a house home. Even though I am beginning to doubt the reality of Santa Claus, my two younger sisters are adamant believers. I am not one to spoil such a wonderful feeling.

As my Dad enters, giving us each some sort of tap on the head, or a hug, we are instructed to seat ourselves around the table. My sisters are buzzing with things that they believe my Dad MUST hear right away. Dad simply quiets them in order for grace to begin. After a simple, but well thought out grace, void of specific instructions for God, but chalk full of thanks, we begin to eat. Shelly, my youngest sister, is telling Dad of her elf sightings while Kara is attempting to think of some fable that will top Shelly's. Mom at some point or another is able to inform Dad of the here's and there's of what the household needs in the next couple of days while I drum up the courage needed to mention the attic. Finally, tired of listening to my sisters and waiting for a pause, I just come flat out with it.

"Dad, can we look at some of Great Grandpa's stuff in the attic tonight?"

"Not tonight," he answers in just the right voice so that I know not to ask again, or anytime soon for that matter.

Later, while lying in my room I contemplate whether or not I should pursue the matter on my own. Deciding to remain brave and steadfast in my quest, I watch the clock in anticipation of midnight. By midnight I know that my parents will be fast asleep, giving me the perfect opportunity to continue my adventure into the attic. My little bedside alarm clock reaches 11:45 and I decide that now is the perfect time. I exit my room and walk along the walls being careful not to step on the specific parts of the old wooden floor that are certain to send creaks throughout the house. Once again I face the door. Giving perfectly timed and careful tugs, the layers of paint begin to give. On the fifth tug the paint cracks loudly and the hinges make the unmistakable creak that is usually associated with a horror movie. I hesitate for a second making sure that my entrance into our own family time capsule did not awaken the authorities. My heart is now beating so fast and so loud that I am afraid anyone within a mile can hear it. Regardless, I squeeze through the small space and begin up the stairs full of dust and cobwebs. My hand searches carefully along the walls feeling for a light switch that shows itself near the top of the short staircase. With extreme caution I flick the switch. A short buzzing sound and a couple of flickers later the small attic light hanging at the end of a wire in the middle of the room gives life to piles of furniture and books, all covered in generations of dust and enough cobwebs to tie me in. Again I stop short in order to detect any noise from my parents' room. The eerie settling of the house gives proof that everyone is asleep. In awe of the undiscovered, I am knee deep in wonderment. Carefully I make my way to a pile of suitcases that may hold the treasures I am searching for. Passing a rocking chair, my foot hits a place in the floor sending a shriek across the attic. I freeze, checking for noise from below which proves difficult due to the constant beating of my little heart.

When all seems clear I reach the suitcases and begin searching their contents, revealing only stiff moth-eaten clothes. Disappointed by my initial find I begin to lift the second suitcase from the top of the pile. This one seems interesting because of its extreme weight, which requires all of my strength in order to set it on the floor. Opening the case proves my effort useless because it contains only old books. A second thought passes my mind. I suddenly remember a story that my Grandmother once told me about an old house that was being condemned when she was a child. She and a couple of her friends when curiously looking through the house came across an old bookcase. Searching through the books proved fruitful because several contained money hidden within. Looking for the same rewards I begin flipping the pages. Book after book gives evidence of no such luck. I then come across a small book with no writing on its cover. Opening its dusty pages I find myself staring at a hand drawn picture of a rather large, old bearded man.

Labeling this as my treasure for the first expedition, I make my way out of the attic. Down the stairs I carefully close the door which now gives even louder creaks than my opening of it. Being too impatient for caution, I simply gather up the paint chips that fell and enter my room satisfied with my discovery.

The next morning I awake astonished at myself for the great courage, or utter craziness, I displayed the night before. Until now I hadn't prepared to suffer the consequences of my actions. I begin walking downstairs in order to get a feel for the situation. By now, 9:30, my Dad is at work and my Mom is doing laundry and dealing with my sisters. I sit at the kitchen table with a bowl of cereal and wait for my Mom to enter the room. In the middle of a bite she enters and says, "Good morning." I return her greeting and detect no hint of trouble. Therefore I finish my cereal and return to my room in order to thumb through my discovery.

Still in my pajama pants and T-shirt I walk into my room, sit on my bed, and begin with the first page…

The North Pole

1892

The account of the expedition

by: George Platt

May 18, 1892, my team of three begins our expedition

into the North Pole. Now 5:00 in the morning we leave

Ellesmere Island in the Arctic Ocean. From Ellesmere

my expedition officially begins. We three are using a

combination of dogsleds and skis. Our sleds are loaded

with only the necessities; beef, fish, and fat for both K-9

and Homo-Sapien. Each of the three sleds weighs over

300 pounds, a right heavy pack for ten dogs per sled.

The rest of the sleds' weight results from cooking

utensils, tent, sleep bags, one American flag, and fire

logs. The fire logs are fairly light and are to be used

simultaneously for cooking and melting snow for

drinking water. If frozen waterways are close enough

we will gather water by making holes in the ice and dragging the filled bottles back to camp on the sleds.

The sled dogs are a mix of Retriever, Hound, Shepherd, Siberian Husky, Saluki, Cattle Dog and whatever else decided at one time or another to jump the fence. The dogs each weigh just under 100 pounds. The thing that amazes me is their spirit. If it were put to a contest I believe that the sled dog would win the enthusiasm reward over any other animal. Although the dogs are bred for strength and endurance, this land will push the limits of both. As soon as we pick up their harnesses they begin barking and dancing just at the thought of leading our sleds around. Back in Michigan, where we trained with and bought the dogs, we were told to keep our fingers clear of the harnesses when hitching the dogs to the sled. Many broken fingers have resulted from the failure to do so because the dogs begin pulling as soon as they think it's time. When they begin we are shot from 0 to 20 miles per hour in a single bound. Many men have been left behind as the dogs bark and scream while following their own directions.

I, George Platt, now twenty-seven, am currently lying on my bag in our tent shortly after finishing dinner with the rest of the crew. A dinner consisting of beef and potatoes. Traveling this time of year is not so bad due to the 24 hours of daylight. Which, on the other hand, tends to leave our bodies in disarray on account of our internal clocks being used to waking at daylight, and sleeping not long after dark. Instead, the sun simply travels in a circle above our heads, never setting.

May 19

After a day like this we begin to wonder why. Why men do such things as this; why we constantly wonder what is up there; or what is under this? God sure knew that if he were to make a place with nothing but snow, ice, and unbearable temperatures that one day man would say, "I'm going to test that old man's creation." After only two days I am talking of the unbearability of this place. If I do not continue, I return home having failed. Worst of all, God will laugh at me saying, "see I told you." So, I guess most of me is doing it for everyone *else, for the pleasure and anticipation of fame and the fear of failure. In the beginning, however, I was to do this purely for me, regardless of my wife and family's opinions of such an endeavor. I am genuinely curious as to what lies ahead. I am most curious as to what, and how much, stamina lives beneath my flesh.*

May 20

Averaging twenty to twenty-five miles a day we are now about 420 miles from the Pole. Leaving us about two and a half to three weeks from our goal. Today nothing unusual happened. In fact I am now experiencing a little anxiety. I am a whole three weeks away, stuck in this boring desolate white land, with a wind-chill factor of 50 below zero, cold enough to frostbite bare skin in minutes. The dogs are working out better than we imagined. Although we trained with them an entire winter near the Great Lakes I am still getting used to their individual personalities. The smartest two dogs are the lead. Next come the swing dogs who are responsible for easing the team around corners and preventing the entire team from turning at once. The next four dogs are what we refer to simply as team dogs, then come the two pullers and, last, the wheel dogs. The wheel dogs are the toughest, the ones who absorb the sudden starts and stops of the sled. I am now lying in the tent admiring these dogs as they sleep. The dogs do not lay awake long and they generate a lot of heat, which is nice. After a dinner of fish, bread, and chocolate, I am going to sleep under another night sky of light and awake to another day of white.

At this point the diary needed to be postponed for two reasons. One, a ten year-old has the attention span of a gnat. Two, the inches of snow and several hours of daylight left opportunities that far out-shadowed reading. Before I began to change into my required snow gear I had to take one more look at the pictures contained within the strange diary. The first picture is of the arctic landscape, the second of the tent and dogsleds outside. Then, the writing changes to ink and there is the picture of the old bearded man I saw last night, followed by several drawings of large houses. Against my natural urges to read the pages that follow close to the illustration of the bearded man I resisted. If it were not my Great-

Grandfather's diary I probably would have just cut to the thick of the matter. However, this man obviously wanted his account read. Otherwise, why write it? So I resolved to read the entire diary page by page, the way it was experienced by the writer.

After I was dressed in all of my gear I hurried downstairs, yelled my pending location to my Mom on the way out the door, and off I went. Joining my friends on a hill located about a half mile behind my house, I raced to

grab a free sled. We used to leave the sleds on the hill during the winter months. Otherwise, we would have had to drag them throughout the woods back to our houses each and every day (which, incidentally, my Dad thinks is what should be done in order to, "properly take care of one's possessions.")

Of course, before I could actually begin sledding I had to give the guys the required explanations as to my tardiness. You see, a boy's play time, a teenager's as well, is serious business. If one is ever late to such activities then a serious explanation is necessary. A real smart-ellic could always tell the group to "mind their own business" when asked for the all-important required explanations, but in the end that smart-ellic gets his. Whether it be by eventual snowball fight or, worst of all, the constant needling. The group, if still feeling an explanation of tardiness necessary, can resort to the unscrupulous act of accusation. When the opponent is faced with many firing accusations, such as, " What, did you have to read to your sisters, or fold laundry?" Too many of those and anyone would have to give in and at least make up a false excuse. So I have always found it better to just face up at the start.

"Well, Benny, where were you," fired that annoying little Jim Stanley.

"I had to help my Dad change a tire on his truck," I fired back.

"It took you that long to change a tire with your Dad?" back-fired Sammy Snute.

"Well, there were three flat tires," I answered with every intent of ending all of this in order to continue our work. I succeeded, although I must admit that I really wanted to tell them the truth.

After an exhaustive sledding excursion we returned home for dinner. Walking back through the woods I remembered the diary and sped up. Entering the door I stopped, removed my snow gear, and ran up to my room. Still somewhat exhausted I flipped to the various drawings before picking up where I had left off. The picture that still continued to hold my attention was the one of the old man.

May 21

More of the same--around lunch my fellow explorers talked of quitting. These grown men harbor ideas of giving up while the dogs still require the sled hook just to keep us from loosing the sleds. [The sled hook is a rather large piece of metal and is attached to the back of the sled to allow the men to secure it into the packed snow so that the excitement of the dogs doesn't leave their gear wondering widely throughout the North Pole without them]. *Questions of our preparedness were also raised today. With 400 miles ahead, and over two weeks left, they wondered out loud if we could sustain such conditions. I loudly dismissed such talk. I then went on to express my deep feelings about this expedition. I talked of our fame in only a month or so when we return to the states with pictures of ourselves as the first to stand at the North Pole. "Men," I said, "this will separate us from those who could only attempt at what will be our success." And so on, in the end just another gumption speech, which I then realized will need further backing as the trip continues.*

By dinner the men didn't need much more of an initiative talk. I guess as we got under way they thought of the fame and satisfaction of our return as successful explorers. Such mental pictures help us deal with the plain white canvas. I must say, I thought we all equally wanted this. Today's short talk proved otherwise. Of course, wanting and doing are as different as a nun and a drunk. Such circumstances force me to assume my new duty as the group's vocal ambition. To be honest, I couldn't care if I had to be the group's chorister, chaplain, and cook. I would gladly assume such responsibility in order to achieve this goal.

With over two weeks of more of the same certainly leaves room for mutiny. I now wish that I had brought a chess board along, instead of only cards.

Returning downstairs, lest any suspicion arise, I sat myself in front of the TV just in time for some *Dukes of Hazzard.* For one reason or another, or perhaps none in particular, I remembered my Grandmother talking of that "crazy old fool" I call my Great Grandfather. I also remembered my Aunt talking of his various trips, along with a smidgen of a conversation concerning the North Pole. For some reason the man was more times than not dismissed as a "crazy old so-and-so." Although he was loved by all who mentioned him, and every picture of him revealed his smiling face, he, for unknown reasons to me, was not regarded seriously in all respects. Stories that were told by him were called just that, stories. The thing about stories is that they are usually grounded on some basis of truth. The storyteller's imagination and desire to shock weave that little ball of truth into a remarkable quilt. The patterns and size of that quilt can change over time, as the story is retold. The truth is still in there, that base never totally disappears which is why it is important to respect such stories, for their base of truth and for the artist who weaved that simple truth into the wonderful quilt that it becomes. That quilt will be rewoven, cut, and added to as time goes on and it is handed from quilter to quilter, but in the end that little ball of truth is still in there.

With only two days until Christmas Eve, the evening carried me from *the Duke boys* to the dinner table. As our meal moved on were alerted as to some goings on outside by our dog Bucket. By the way, he was named Bucket because when my Dad and I went to pick him up at a family friend's house, he, only a small black dot, hid himself in a metal bucket. My sisters and I rushed to the kitchen window and saw our Aunt Katherine getting out of her Valiant. The excitement that comes with such a visit, one that usually includes candy, poured into my aunt's arms as she entered the kitchen door. Once the greetings were over, my Dad inquired as to his sister's unexpected visit. Only living about forty minutes away she said that she wanted to stop by and see the excitement that builds in us before Christmas. She then handed us little boxes of fudge. Of course I could not open the box until after I finished dinner but I knew what it contained. There are those little certainties that life holds, Easter brings a new suit, Thanksgiving brings turkey, and Christmas brings those little boxes containing the best fudge since its invention.

Once the excitement settled I knew that I was seated at the perfect opportunity for my burning question. "I want to hear about Great-Grandpa," I stated.

My Dad looked and asked, "well, what do you want to know?" You see this is the perfect family for such questions, we are Virginians, and as such we love history, both national and family, especially family. We love to talk in tones of remembrance.

"I want to know about his expeditions, especially the North Pole," I returned.

"Well," my Aunt interjected, "he was quite the adventurer." She went on, "when he was in his twenties he and some other gentlemen set out to be the first to set foot on the Pole."

"Or so he said," my Dad explained.

My Aunt continued, "after about one and a half weeks I guess the other men abandoned him." Of course he was overcome with the desire to continue on. After another four days he reached the Pole. "The story gets complicated around this point," she paused and looked to my father.

"Well, he said that he passed out from exhaustion and was discovered a day later," my Dad continued.

"Discovered by who?" I asked.

"By none other than Santa Claus," my Aunt said with great satisfaction. My sisters and I now showed eyes the size of tennis balls,

"Santa Claus?" we exclaimed together.

"Oh yes, Santa took him into his village and took care of him," my Aunt stated. "Your Great Grandfather is the only man to have seen Santa's village."

Several ridiculous questions from my sisters followed. All I knew was I could not wait to get back to the journal. I wanted so badly to reveal it, but I also knew that trouble would follow, so I continued with my secret. After dinner and my Aunt's visit, I returned to the diary. Knowing in a nutshell what happened up to a point from the discussion at dinner, I flipped pages until I found where my Great Grandfather was left alone.

May 31

Today, the roughest of my life to date. At lunch my friends told me that they would no longer continue. Directly ahead of us lay a massive pressure ridge. The ridge appears miles wide and at least 30 feet tall. [Pressure ridges form when shifting plates of polar ice slam into one another, forming a wall]. *This, along with the elements and struggle, not to mention the strict dietary budget we are on, forced the others to give up. I pleaded and gave as many speeches as my energy would allow. I do not understand how someone could give up when we have only about three or five days to our destination, especially when we have come this far. I do not understand how they could leave me.*

They begged me to go home with them but I refused. I now own all the spoils of this expedition when I return successful. They, the weak, return failures. They attempted to rationalize with me; I, of course, counter-rationalized. In the end I sat on my dogsled, watching them head South. They took the tent, but left me with the majority of the food. I had left a good team of strong dogs, a strong sled, food, and every extremity frostbitten beyond repair. But I was also left with a strong will to finish what I started. I watched as they disappeared into the distance. Immediately I was lonelier than I ever imagined. I thought of chasing after them and being in my warm home in just over three weeks. Otherwise I had about three or five days ahead, and about a three week return to Ellesmere, all on my own.

I packed up, wanting to cry in my loneliness, but I continued on. I made my way around the ridge with great difficulty. The difficulty resulted from the minor ridges that are created around the main one. Each one required the dogs and I to maneuver the sled either over or around it. After reaching the other side I camped directly beside the gigantic ridge. I was extremely weak, and I must admit the thought of returning to the other side of that ridge and catching up to the other men now seamed very tempting. Instead I unhooked the dogs and stretched canvas over the sled, the dogs, and I. As miserable as conditions were I had no choice but to fall asleep from exhaustion.

June 1

Today I continued on, thinking only happy thoughts. I told jokes to the dogs and, as far as relativity goes, ate like a king, due to the fact that I had plenty of food for now and the return trip. I also fed the dogs well, payment for not quitting on me. I thought of celebrating the Fourth of July as sort of a celebrity. I thought of planting the Stars and Stripes firmly in the ground, right on the North Pole. Now I sleep.

June 2

Awoken by passion, I pushed my growing weakness into that part of my brain that only the inventor knows exists. Today anoth

The words stopped here. This must be where he passed out I thought. I flipped another page and continued.

Date unknown

From this point on, whoever the reader is may think me a disillusioned fool, a crazed lunatic. The fact is that what I write is nothing but God's truth, and when I return home I will say nothing to the contrary, even to the day I die. I awoke in a large wooden bed with intricate carvings adorning the headboard. The sheets were the softest my hands have ever touched. The comforter, also of a fine material, was woven in a fascinating and wonderful pattern of snowflakes. The room was large, with a dresser across the room from the bed. Beside the dresser stood a large bookshelf with many beautifully bound books. Some bound in leather and others in brightly colored cloth. The closet was full of clothes from what seemed to be every period in history. I noticed ladies' dresses from what must have been the fifteenth century and mens' clothing that looked like what Thomas Jefferson would have worn. A note on the nightstand, written by a steady and meticulous hand read...

In-between the next page was this note…

Hello George

I found you about 22 miles
South of here. You were discovered
due to the loud barking of
your sled dogs who are in the
barn warm and well fed.
Please make yourself at home.
You may clean up and put on
any clothes that appeal to you.
My wife can usually be found
around the kitchen. She will be
happy to fix anything you would
like to eat.
I labeled the way to the kitchen
with notes on the walls so you
will not get lost.
Again, My House is Your House
Your Old Friend
Sb

I nearly jumped off my bed. Santa Claus, Santa Claus I shouted, that is what the initials S.C. stands for. Then I realized my surroundings and calmed a bit for fear of trouble from below. I could not believe that I held in my hand a letter from Santa Claus. My Great Grandfather really did meet, not only meet, but slept in Santa's house. Wow, I could not contain myself, my heart racing I knew that this information could no longer be kept secret. Regardless of the trouble I may find myself in, I resolved to tell the world tomorrow. As for that moment, I tried, and you must know I really had to try, to settle down in order to further research this important archeological find.

I stood for about fifteen minutes just staring out of my bedroom window at the snow that fell in front of the light that was fixed above the shed door. All the while I held the note in my hand. So badly I wanted to just grip it as hard as I could but then I would destroy such an important document. As my heartbeat settled I was staring up at the moon, almost calm I began realizing that within a matter of seconds I was again a believer in Santa Claus. Just days ago I was a doubter, now a firm believer. A belief so solid that nothing, nothing at all could strip it from me. What a wonderful feeling it is to believe in something so good.

I knew that I had to settle down and finish my Great Grandfather's journal, then in the morning alert the presses. SANTA EXISTS!!!, SANTA EXISTS!!!! I would exclaim. But I had to finish, knowing that it would only get better. I flipped through the pages and briefly looked at the drawings. I opened the book jacket to find three signatures on the back cover. The first was my Great Grandfather's, the second Jonathan something (I couldn't make out the last name), and the third was Stephen Christopher. Stephen Christopher, S.C., Stephen Christopher not Santa Claus. My heart went from top speed to a steady slow beat. An involuntary frown found its way onto my face, I sat on my bed and my back slumped. After suffering through several moments of disappointment I decided to read on.

The more I awoke I noticed an extreme pain in my hands and feet. Both were bandaged, so I carefully unwrapped the cloth to find the tips of my toes and feet coal black in color. I had the worst frostbite I had ever seen. While the pain was extreme only the tips were dead, I was amazed that I suffered only this.

I cleaned myself in the bathroom that connected to the bedroom. The bathroom was huge with every scent and shape of soap imaginable. After the most relaxing bath I have every taken I picked out a nice pair of pants and shirt, and a pair of leather boots. I then cleaned whatever mess I created and made the bed. Before I headed toward the kitchen I looked out of the window and into the outside world. There were several nice looking, rather large buildings about twenty feet from my window. The largest was red brick with dark green shutters. The building was three stories tall and took up several acres. The roof was an A-frame with three large smokestacks and six chimneys, all which had smoke pouring out.

I walked out of the bedroom to a long hallway. The ceilings were thirteen feet tall and I noticed a note at the end of the hallway. The note instructed me to take a left and go down the stairs. I looked left into a large room with couches and a fireplace as tall as me. I turned left and went down the stairs. The walls everywhere were adorned with pictures. There were paintings, drawings, and pictures of people and places. At the bottom of the staircase was another note that informed me that the kitchen was the last room after I turned left and went straight. The smell of chocolate chip cookies filled my senses and made the directional notes unnecessary. Never before in my life had I felt so comfortable in such a strange place.

I took a left and passed many large rooms. One appeared to be an office with a huge desk made of oak. The legs were carved like pine trees and books and maps were all over the place. I walked up to the kitchen and looked around the room. Noticing no one, I walked in to hear a women bid me goodmorning. Looking to my left I saw a somewhat elderly women in an apron standing at the sink. She took off her apron and gave me a hug, looked me up and down and said, "Well George, you have certainly grown into a nice looking man, how are you doing?"

"Good," I responded.

"Well sit down and have some breakfast," she said as she motioned to a table across from the kitchen island. I sat at the round table with my back to a large bay window.

I began, "You know I..."

She said, "I know George, I know." She continued while cooking, "My husband found you and brought you back here early yesterday morning." My husband is working right now but he should be back in a couple of hours for lunch, so please make yourself at home."

I still questioned, "But what do y'all do here in the middle of nowhere?"

"Well in the back of your head you know who lives at the North Pole," she stated.

"You, you mean I am at the North Pole?" I eagerly questioned.

"Yes, you sure are," she returned. I could not believe so many things at this point in the adventure. For one, I made it to the North Pole; for two, could she be implying that I am at the home of Santa Claus?

As she brought me a plate of plump and steaming biscuits, along with bacon, scrambled eggs and blueberry jam, coupled with a tall glass of orange juice, I wanted to ask her name. "Ma'am, you know my name but I..."

"Mrs. Claus." She returned as I fell out of my chair spilling orange juice all over me. With many apologies we cleaned the mess as I made my way back into the seat.

"Mrs. Claus, well Mrs. Claus I must say that there was a time when I believed in this place, now as I sit in this huge house I am on the verge of reaffirming my faith," I stated.

"Well it's about time you did George," she returned with a smile.

I sat there as she went on about her business and we talked of my explorations. After finishing an excellent breakfast, she brought me a plate of fresh chocolate chip cookies and a tall glass of milk. As I finished she once again told me to make myself at home and said that I may wonder around as I wish. She gave me the locations of such rooms as the library and the game room. I thanked her profusely and told her that I would like to see the dogs and check on my gear. She said that *her husband would be glad to take me outside when he comes in for lunch if I didn't mind waiting. I agreed and set out for a nap because I was still worn out from such a long ordeal of getting wherever I was. I found the library, looked around the huge room full of pictures, nice furniture, desks, maps and thousands of books. I found a copy of <u>A Christmas Carol</u>, and opened to the first page to find it signed by Charles Dickens, the inscription read...*

To the oldest and best friend the world has ever known

your friend, Charles Dickens.

"George, George, wake up, would you like some lunch." I sat up on the couch, rubbed my eyes and saw Mrs. Claus standing above me. Again she said, "Sorry to wake you but I wondered if you would like a little lunch and then maybe check on your dogs."

"Yes, yes I would thank you, is, is your husband around?" I questioned.

"Yes, he is in his office," she said. She helped me up and we went down the hallway, she then pointed into the office and told me that he was in there, and that lunch would be ready shortly. She smiled and continued walking toward the kitchen. I peered in and saw the back of a rather plump man with white hair standing in front of a window twice as tall as him. He was looking at a book or something. I knocked on the opened door and he turned to face me. I fell against the door a little and found my heart beating a mile a minute. My palms became sweaty and I momentarily lost all ability to speak.

"George, George am I glad to see you, come in," he said as he motioned towards a chair on my side of his desk. I slowly made my way to the seat. He put out his hand and gave me a very firm handshake.

I looked into his bright blue sparkling eyes and smiled, I could do nothing else. No other reaction was available to me; I just stood there and smiled. His beard was full and whiter than the whitest snow, his smile larger and warmer than any I have ever seen. I knew that I was looking directly at Santa Claus. There was no *room for doubt; I knew that as much as I know my name, this was Santa Claus. I couldn't move an inch; I just stood there and smiled. He walked around the desk and sat in his large leather chair and again motioned for me to sit. I made it to the seat all the while carrying the greatest smile my face would allow, it was all I could do. Being in the presence of Santa does that to a person.*

As I sat down he said, "How are you doing," in a very warming tone, such that I forgot a lifetime of pains and worries.

"Good, great, I am just fine," I said in a very shaky, nervous voice. It was like I was a child again, too nervous to approach the man who used to come into my very own living room wearing soot from my chimney. Yet, he stood right in front of me with a red button up shirt and gray wool pants that were held up with dark green suspenders. Sawdust was stuck to the bottom of his pants and covered his old leather work boots. He told me that my dogs were just fine, that they are in the barn playing with his dogs. He said that he repaired my sled and made some minor improvements to it. He then said that he knew I would be anxious to get home but that he wished I would stay a while. He cleaned up his desk a little that was full of maps and journals and stacks of letters.

"Are those letters from children?" I asked

"Yes, they sure are, they write year-round, inviting me to birthday parties and sleep-overs. Many people wonder why I rarely write back, to tell the truth I really wish that I could, I wish that I had the time to make it to all of their wonderful parties."

I told him that I had a million and one questions for him. I told him that I wanted to see everything. Of course in his deep booming voice, and with a laugh that could only be described as jolly, he told me that he couldn't show me everything. The thing is that I understood. As badly as I wanted to see the entire village I knew that it was not my place to nose around. As an explorer I go where I am told I cannot. I go where others have not, but when he told me that I could not, I understood, although it went against my natural grain. I would not dream of going against his wishes. As children we are told to be asleep on Christmas Eve before it gets too late, and we are, we know why, it's an unwritten rule.

Mrs. Claus called us to lunch. He got up from his desk and motioned me toward the door. "I sure hope that you are hungry George," he said as we walked down the hall toward the kitchen.

"Sir I have not stopped eating since I woke up," I responded, he chuckled.

As we approached the kitchen a myriad of smells filled our heads. We sat down at the kitchen table to large bowls of clam chowder, biscuits and crackers. I was asked by Mrs. Claus what I would like to drink and I said that water would be fine. As she sat down we began eating. I ate slowly with a very nervous stomach. I could not get over the fact that I was sitting at the kitchen table of the Clauses. I saw their happy faces and their occasional smiles directed at me and knew that they were also happy to have me there. Although I was no saint or any type of celebrity, I figured that just having company was a seldom and beautiful occurrence in their lives. I made a conscience effort to keep myself from staring at Santa. I routinely attempted to study his face as I looked out of the corner of my eye. During one bite of chowder I lowered my chin closer to the bowl and with my head down a glance at Santa's hands turned into a stare. I quickly realized that my head was near the bowl for too long and that any effort I put into concealing my gazes was lost. I did notice that his hands were those of a strong man. They were the hands of a worker. They reminded me of my Dad's hands. The fingers were meaty and plump and full of scars and scrapes. The fingernails were chipped off in places and hid dirt in others. The back of his hand was firm and ready for labor as the blood vessels protruded outward suggesting a day's work had been done already.

After several moments of silence he said, "George, after we eat would you like to go to the barn and check on your dogs?"

"Oh, yes that would be just fine, thank you," I responded. I want to see everything, I thought to myself. I knew inside that such a trip included seeing the reindeer. We discussed my family then sat for a while before getting up to see the barn. I wanted to ask so many questions but held back, there are things that I cannot know, coupled with the fact that I didn't want to pry.

I was instructed to find a coat that I liked from the hall closet. We left through the kitchen door as Mrs. Claus continued to clean up from lunch. The wind was blowing terribly as we made our way past several large brick buildings that had smoke pouring out of the smokestacks. The barn was a round building, two stories tall, and looked to be about a half mile in diameter. It was constructed of dark green cinder blocks with windows all around. We opened the large thick wooden doors and the smell of hay filled my nose. Entering I heard my dogs begin barking in excitement. As my eyes somewhat adjusted I saw my whole team of dogs running full speed toward me, they began jumping on me and licked my hands. I knelt down almost in tears; they were so happy to see me they could not contain themselves. Santa knelt down beside me and they immediately showed him the same attention.

Looking around I noticed about twenty reindeer, some adults and several little ones. There were about thirty separate stalls around the walls of the barn. All of the reindeer began walking toward us. Santa told me that they were coming to say hello to the new visitor. They came up to me very calmly and sniffed and rubbed their soft noses on me.

The barn that I was standing in was remarkable. The floor was made of some type of soft wood, covered in a layer of hay. The center of the round building held a large circular fireplace with a chimney that rose through the tall ceiling. The barn was plenty large for exercise and running. While looking around I heard Santa say,

"Oh no, Cupid not now, George is our guest." I looked over to him and he explained that several of the reindeer like playing jokes on people. He informed me that their favorite is to sneak behind someone and lay down while another reindeer walks towards the person. The person then backs up a little and falls over the reindeer lying behind them. He said that they were planning that one for me. I thanked him for warning me.

I then walked over to check on my gear and the sled that Santa worked on. To my sudden astonishment I noticed the most famous reindeer of all. Yes, it was Rudolf, no doubt about it. He was walking toward me from the other side of the fireplace. His nose was a dull red, but began to glow the closer he got to me. I reached out to pet him and his nose was glowing a bright, bright red. As I began petting him and telling him just how famous he was I almost started crying. To stop from doing so I looked over to Santa who was checking on all of his reindeer. I looked back at Rudolf and quietly asked him how he got his red nose. He just pranced and rubbed his nose on me while I petted him.

The reader must understand that this day was without a doubt the most remarkable of my life. While reading this you must not say to yourself for even a second that I was not struck with all of the excitement that a man can muster, I was. I am writing this while I lay in bed before I try and sleep which will, no doubt, be difficult due to being in such an exciting and magical place. I try to convey the excitement that filled every inch of my body onto paper so that you may feel it. While an impossible task, I must attempt it. As for now it doesn't look like I'll be getting to sleep tonight.

My sled had many improvements. The runners were redone with stronger wood and polished metal bases. The hand bars were replaced with a thicker, lighter wood that was carved in intricate patterns of trees, while the handle was woven with a thick, soft fabric. My pack was replaced with a larger one done in a very strong fabric that I could not readily identify. The back of it was stitched in a large white snowflake above which was written "George Platt-North Pole." I also found a large tent that could be packed into a bag no longer than my

forearm and no wider than my leg. I looked it all over,
which was placed beside my old assembly of gear and I
imagined a Christmas tree standing tall above it all.

"Well I guess that you like it all," he said.

"You did all of this while I was sleeping for that short
time?" I asked.

He responded by telling me that he could have done
much more, and still would, if I could think of anything
else that I would need or like. I thanked him more than I
have ever thanked a person before. What more could I
need, this gear was better than any I have ever heard of;
with such gear I could take on any earthly obstacle that
God chose to lay before me.

After my dogs settled and the reindeer were tended to,
we left the barn. I asked what I was allowed to see and
told him what he already knew, that I wanted to see it
all, every inch of it. Of course I told him that I knew my
request could not be honored and I respected that fact. I
could tell that he wanted to show me everything, just to
see my joy and astonishment. There is one thing that
Santa loves to see in others, and that is joy. He thrives
on smiles. He simply said, "George, tomorrow is

another day." Uncertain as to how long I should stay without overstaying my welcome, several things entered my mind. One was that I wanted to stay forever, another was that there were those worried about me suffering the elements alone, and finally, I was also eager to return home victorious, in more ways than one.

We walked back into the house again through the kitchen door to be greeted by Mrs. Claus. She asked what I thought of the improvements on my gear. I gave my very appreciative response and was then told that Santa had to go to work and that I was once again to make myself at home. I returned to the library to look over the many great literary works, many of which were signed by the author.

Before long, dinner was called and we again sat around the dinner table. We ate very juicy and perfectly seasoned steaks with sweet potatoes and green beans. "Very American," I thought to myself. During my break in the library I resolved to ask as many questions as I could because I knew that I would be leaving soon.

"Do y'all usually eat such American type dishes," I asked.

"Well, he's a meat and potatoes type of guy, but we do enjoy foods of the world, in fact tomorrow I was thinking of eating Chinese," Mrs. Claus responded.

I made sure to tell her how wonderful everything was, right down to the biscuits. She told me that since I was from Virginia that she also thought it would make me feel at home to eat such Southern meals. I once again told her how thankful I was.

Then I was overcome with the urge to ask a million questions at once, just like an eager child. "How did Rudolf's nose get red, which building is your workshop, where are the elves?" I asked. Santa looked over to me with a slight smile and told me that we could talk of such things after dinner. After dinner I thought, how could I wait that long, I had a lifetime's worth of questions.

After dinner Santa said that he had to run back to the workshop for a short time and that I could do as I please. He assured me that he would be back shortly. I ran to my room and grabbed several pieces of paper out of my diary. Sitting back at the dinner table I began writing down my questions, to be sure that I didn't forget anything important, or repeat the same questions. Mrs.

Claus asked what I was doing and I told her that I was writing down all of my questions and asked if she thought Santa would mind. She assured me that he loves such questions,

"Children all over the world ask him their very important questions and he sometimes tells me some of them, and I must say that they are very entertaining. And George, he always answers them truthfully, letting you know what you cannot know."

"What a wonderful man," I said, not exactly to her, I just said it outloud.

She turned to me and smiled. She was cooking again, so I began with one of my questions.

"Do you always spend so much time cooking?"

"Oh yes, right now I am making more chocolate chip cookies. It takes a lot of work for everyone here to keep up. I am constantly cooking and Santa is constantly in the workshops." Wow I thought, these questions are going great.

Within a short time Santa returned and we went into

his office. He carefully filled his pipe with a graceful

ease while sitting back in great satisfaction. When the pipe was filled he twisted his thumb around the bowl and compacted the ingredients with such a serious look on his face. In moments the office filled with a spicy pipe smoke, a welcoming and relaxed feeling developed.

"Well George, let me begin with your first question."

He went on to tell me that Rudolf was not exactly his strongest reindeer in the beginning. So here I begin with Santa's reindeer...

Santa's Reindeer

Rudolf was a little weaker than most of the other reindeer. Therefore he was unable to fly on Christmas

Eve, which is, by the way, every reindeer's most fervent wish. Santa said that he was astonished at Rudolf's courage and will power. He tried and tried to be as strong as the others. He would practice day in and day out. Then on one stormy, nasty night Rudolf decided that he didn't want to be inside the barn with the others, so he went outside to practice flying in bad weather. Of course the other reindeer warned him against it but he was determined to fly on the next Christmas Eve, just as he was determined on the previous years. Well, on this particular night he did not return to the barn. The next morning Santa said that he was notified of the emergency. Santa also made it clear that I understand just how smart these reindeer are. He said that they have superb senses of direction in all types of weather. They are extremely strong, and have to be in order to sustain such a trying flight. He laughed and said that they cannot speak, but are very good at letting him know what they would say if they could talk.

So on that morning the reindeer and Santa set out to find Rudolf. Santa said that he found Rudolf about three miles east of the barn lying on the ground. He ran over to him, loaded him on the sled, and the reindeer pulled the sled back to the barn in a matter of seconds. He laid Rudolf onto a bed in the barn and began to revive him. He said that his heart was still beating so he laid warm blankets on him in order to warm his shivering body. The other reindeer licked Rudolf's face in order to bring him back. Santa said that the unusual thing was that Rudolf's nose was a sort of dark red color. In a little while Rudolf did slowly regain strength and as he did his nose began to glow causing the others to jump back in astonishment. It turned out Rudolf flew through an electrical storm late that night. Now Rudolf's nose glows when he gets excited and he can even make it glow on command. Then Santa said, "And you know how the song goes."

"So George, does that answer your question?" Santa asked.

"Oh yes, yes it does thank you," I said. I then asked if I could continue with some more questions.

The Elves

With reservation I inquired into the realm of the magic

little people. As soon as the question left my lips he

laughed and asked why I was so scared of such a

question. He informed that one of the top three questions that children ask is about the elves. "Yes, oh yes, and without them I would not get anywhere," he said about the elves existence.

My next question was why I have yet to see any, and then I wondered if I could be introduced. My heart pounding harder and harder as I asked such a question. I tried to imagine shaking their little hands and witnessing their around the clock work that all children dream of. "Well George, the elves are a little different than most people, for one, they have magic, and second, they are rarely ever seen by those other than myself and Mrs. Claus," he replied.

He went on to tell me that he himself had elf blood running through his veins. He said that one can tell an elf apart from other people by these following traits.

1. The elves have very rosy cheeks, year round, regardless of the temperature.

2. The elves are very mischievous, and they love playing jokes.

3. The elves do in fact have the proverbial pointy ears, which they are somewhat self-conscious of.

4. They do posses several magical abilities. They are able to disappear for a short time and reappear somewhere else. They also have excellent hearing, which helps them avoid being seen.

5. They are very strong and have a passion for hard work. Most of them are not in any way lazy, however, many of them do not enjoy being awakened early in the morning.

6. Elves strongly dislike vegetables.

It was made very clear to me, in a nice way of course, that I could not see the workshop. The workshop was a series of the three largest of all buildings, and was where the elves worked on all toy orders, almost around the clock. It was because of the elves that I was prevented from seeing the inside of the workshops. If I *were heard coming Santa said that they would hide*

quicker than I could ever imagine, which would slow

their work. He said that he fully understood my curiosity

concerning the elves, but that the decision was not all

his. The elves just don't like being seen, they prefer to

see you. "In fact there are about a half dozen watching

you right now."

Upon hearing that I spun around in the chair hoping

to catch one, but of course it did not work. He said that

just about every elf at the North Pole has had a look at

me since I arrived because many of them rarely get to

see people. Most of them work year-round, they are the

ones who fill the orders, make the toys, keep the

buildings maintained, and so on. Then there are the

elves that report to him. Finally, there are the elves that

go out into the world and keep an eye on the children.

Those elves report on a child's new interests, how they

are doing in school, how they are treating their families,

and so on. Santa calls these elves the "reporters," they

are reporting back to him and keeping notes constantly.

Santa calls the elves who stay in the North Pole the

"workers," he said that most elves, whether reporters or workers, do work very hard.

I also remembered hearing as a child that many of the elves were very old. To this Santa said that Winsleff, the oldest elf at the North Pole, worked with Apollos De Revoire (Paul Revere's father) at his Boston silversmith shop. Santa stated that Winslef was at least two centuries old at that time. He went on to say that several of the elves are currently in St. Petersburg for several months working with Peter Carl Faberge, he said that they enjoy the detail of such work. I then thought that I would ask Santa his age, he just lowered his chin a little, looked at me above his little bifocals that rested on his nose, and gave a little smirk. I never again asked such a question, and as a word of advice, when you see Santa, you too should avoid that particular question.

When I asked why elves live so much longer than people, Santa simply said, "Because they have elf blood." Which also explains why Santa has lived so long, and I must say on behalf of all of the children, thank goodness. Santa did say this,

"What has kept me on this earth for so long, and will continue to, is the love that emanates from children all over the world. Nothing gives me more energy and life than seeing excitement in a child's eyes."

While Santa said that he loves seeing excitement in a child's eyes more than anything else, he is left out Christmas morning. He does not get to see the joy that is brought to a child by his long Christmas Eve flight. He misses the hugging of dolls and the excitement of toy trains. Instead he goes by detailed accounts brought to him by the reporter elves. After Christmas Eve Santa said that he and the worker elves have several days to relax, which is when the reporter elves work overtime. They travel the world recording the children's reactions that are to be brought back to Santa as quickly as possible. He said that the reporter elves have come to realize how important the stories are to him. When they return several days after Christmas they each cannot wait to tell Santa what they saw. Santa said that one by one as they begin returning he sits with them, usually with milk and cookies, and is told what each child thought of his or her gift. While it would take forever for Santa to hear about every single child's reaction, he does hear most of the stories. He said that the reporter elves, regardless of how exhausted they are, are so excited to give him their news that they sometimes begin speaking in elf gibberish. He said that elves sometimes break into elf gibberish when they become too excited about something. The other elves can sometimes understand the gibberish, but Santa said that he has a very hard time trying to keep up. Which is why the beginning of such story telling sessions takes a while, because the elves require some time to be calmed. Santa did admit that because he cannot wait to hear the stories he is somewhat responsible for their breaking into gibberish. He said that Mrs. Claus is excellent at calming everyone down so that everything can be understood. Milk and chocolate chip cookies are also a big help he said, which, by the way, I noticed is a Claus family cure-all. Of course I don't mind such a wonderful medicine.

The sun began showing itself through my bedroom window. I was beginning to fall asleep, while this was such an exciting thing to read I could barely keep my eyes open. In a matter of minutes I was asleep, knowing that I would show everyone the journal when I awoke.

With some knocking, and "wake up, wake up, it's 12:30," I alerted my Mom that I was up. Getting up, still tired, I looked down at my bed to see the journal. Immediately I was fully awake. I knew that I had some work to do that day. That was the day that my Great Grandpa and I were to become heroes, and Santa was to be proven real. I hurried to get dressed (skipping the part where I brush my teeth, such a tedious task for a person with such important business ahead of him). As I began to rush out of my room I hesitated at the top of the stairs. I puzzled as to how I would tell my Mom. My first instinct was that she would be overcome with joy at my find. But then, then what about the, "Young man, just what were you doing in the attic, you know that you are not supposed to be up there without permission." I concluded that if I were to get in trouble then that was the way it was to be. My Great Grandfather was a brave man and I would have to be too. I had an important historical find in my grips, besides, what child gets in trouble that close to Christmas?

Me, does that answer your question? Yes, I am the child who got in trouble that close to Christmas.

"At this point I don't care what you found in the attic, you set it right there on the table and we'll talk about this when your father comes home," my Mom said. I was then instructed to sit and eat lunch. As my sisters were called in my Mom was pouring vegetable soup into our bowls.

"Why did you sleep in so long?" she asked me.

"Well, I was reading Great Grandpa's journal...," I was saying as I was told that that was quite enough out of me.

My sisters got some type of enjoyment out of seeing me in trouble, and of course they wanted to know why. Their asking my Mom why I was in such trouble got them nowhere. Which left me with a sort of satisfaction. I did something that I was not supposed to, only two people in the room knew what it was, and my sisters weren't included.

"Mom, I know that I wasn't supposed to, but, well, can I please just show you something that is in the journal?" I asked. As she still said no, I could tell that she was awful curious as to what I found. She knew, that I knew, that I would get in trouble if I showed her anything that I found somewhere that I wasn't supposed to be. Which meant to her that the journal held something interesting, not just to a ten-year-old, but because it was written by an interesting, somewhat mysterious relative, it should hold at least a little interest to any Platt.

As lunch came to an end my sisters went about their day of play, and I remained at the kitchen table. My Mom obviously understood why I did what I did. Curiosities drive mankind, those who fail to understand that fail to understand how we came this far, and will continue to go farther. Of course mothers send their boys to school to read about the bravery of George Washington and the courage it took Ben Franklin to fly a kite during a lightning storm. But no mother wants to see her son attempt such acts. As I sat there quietly she picked up the journal and carried it to the table. She sat down and wiped the worn leather cover, smiled a little and looked over at me. I just smiled, things were going well and I was afraid to say anything for fear of incriminating myself further. She opened it and slowly began reading. As the mood on her face glowed, and she looked over at me again, I sheepishly asked if I could show her something. I leaned over and flipped to a drawing of Santa Claus. She gasped a little, and then laughed quietly. "Oh my, what exactly do you think this is?" she said. Knowing that popular opinion concerning my Great Grandfather held that he was a little crazy, eccentric, and all in all a story teller, which left me to consider her question seriously. I knew that she considered the journal as just another rung in the ladder of stories that my Great Grandfather supposedly created. Therefore she also figured that I was putting stock into a diary that was a farce. I told her that I held a firm belief in its truth. Still tired I flung myself onto the couch to contemplate the possibility of the journal being false.

As hard as I tried to think of the journal as nothing more than a story invented only for pleasure, I could not believe it. I knew, as well as you know that nothing like that could ever just be invented, it has to be witnessed, and lived. I peered around the corner to see what I knew I would before I looked, my Mom reading the journal. She looked very serious and intent, a look of total belief. In a little while I would have my first verdict. Then my Father would be home and eventually my Aunt, then Grandma, until the entire jury ruled on the case.

Eventually my Mom finished, leaving me no signs of feeling on the issue. Instead of asking, I waited for the talk that would come when my Dad came home. As Dad entered, several long hours later, my sisters gave the excited greetings that come from youngsters this close to Christmas. Instead I waited anxiously for the journal to come up. As each minute seemed like an hour, I could no longer wait. "Dad, Mom and I have something to show you," I said with excitement.

"Oh yeah, what is that?" he said as he looked at my Mom. I walked to the table and gave him the journal.

He sat down and looked at the cover, opened it slowly and glanced over the first page.

"Where did you find this?" he asked me. As I fumbled around with an answer my Mom saved me by saying that she already talked with me about going into the attic. He then walked into the living room with the journal, sat on the couch and began reading. I sat beside him wanting badly to turn ahead to the good parts, but knew that my patience was required with such a delicate situation.

My Mom worked on dinner while my sisters asked me many questions concerning the journal. They knew that I was somewhat off the hook for whatever trouble I was in earlier. They also knew that Dad was not to be bothered immediately, Mom was cooking, and that left me. I told them that Dad was reading Great Grandpa's journal. I then told them in a quiet and serious tone that it talked of Santa Claus. Their eyes widened and I could see excitement building. I interrupted telling them to keep it quiet until Dad was finished. They understood, and went off by themselves, returning periodically to show me that they were keeping their silence. Dinner was called eventually and my Dad walked silently to the table along with my sisters. I rejected any feelings that told me to continue my patience. "Dad, how far did you get?" I asked.

"Well, to be honest with you I do remember him telling everyone about this expedition, we even have pictures to prove it."

"Along with newspaper clippings," my Mom interjected.

Dad continued, "As for the part about him being discovered by Santa Claus...." My sisters decided to interrupt with a thousand questions, which left my Dad to continue in a fashion that would cater to the two moods being represented at the dinner table -- the serious want of historical knowledge represented by my Mom and I, and the "Tell me about Santa Claus and nothing more" faction represented by my sisters.

"When I was a child I remember my Grandpa telling us many stories about him traveling to the North Pole, and yes, being discovered by Santa Claus," my Dad said. He sometimes told us not to go telling everyone for fear that adults would think of him as nothing more than a story teller. It was very important to him that we believe he was the first man to reach the North Pole, that was what he set out to do. He felt very passionately about his encounter with Santa Claus, and we believed every word of it. The fact is that if he came back telling everyone that he saw Santa Claus then the world would think of him as a fool. So he kept the Santa story within the family, not even telling close friends."

I took advantage of this short silence to ask my Dad if he believed his Grandfather's story. My Dad was silent for a while, I noticed a tear form and slowly make its way down his cheek, he wiped the tear and looked down at his napkin. His voice quivered a little as he tried to say something, he paused again leaving our house with a silence that my ears have yet to deal with.

Our house gave a loud creak that came from upstairs and my Dad looked up, "Yes, yes, I do believe him, I always did and I always will," he said as his face smiled without his mouth even moving. My sisters again showed signs of great excitement without saying much, in a way they understood the seriousness of the situation that I created.

As my Dad slowly made his way through the story, Bucket alerted us to a visitor. My sisters and I jumped up to look out of the kitchen window as we always do when Bucket sounds the alarm. A sort of competition ensued between my sisters and I at that point, the first one to identify the visitor would win. I lost that time because I was last to the window; Aunt Katherine was on her way to the door.

"Merry Christmas Eve Eve," she said upon entering. She handed out little wrapped boxes to each of us along with kisses and hugs. "Right now the elves are working overtime at the North Pole, are you all so exited?" she asked as my sisters answered her question without saying a word. My Dad got up to give her a kiss on the cheek. She sat down as my Mom offered her some dinner. She accepted, "Oh thank you, but only a little please."

As my Mom fixed her a plate my sisters asked if they could go ahead and open their presents. Of course, Aunt Katherine gave the O.K. and they were off. Within milliseconds the floor was adorned with little balls of wrappings and they gave quick "thank you's" as they ran off to play with their new dolls. I unwrapped my box to discover four very nice toy soldiers. I gave thanks and began to set the soldiers on the table and take a closer look. I was not prepared to go play with my new toys just yet because my Aunt would provide new stimulation to the North Pole discussion.

She was eased into the situation by my Father as she ate. My Mom slid the journal over to her. She wiped her mouth, took a drink of water, and began to read. She remained very calm and unsuprised during the whole thing, as if she expected it. She read a little, and was filled in a little by my Father, but I contributed what I could. As the story developed her eyes widened and she gave many, "Oh my's."

"You know, I never doubted it for a second, and I wish that our Grandfather was around so that the children could hear the account from him first hand," she said with beaming pride. My Father nodded in agreement and my Mom smiled, as everyone looked over to me adoringly, I smiled too. We sat there for quite a while looking at the drawings in the journal and talking of Great Grandpa. Eventually my sisters were called in to look at the journal, they were told the story in pieces, mostly because it was difficult for my Dad and Aunt to say too much at once in light of the excitement that was building in their imaginations. I must admit that I was doing a wonderful job of containing my excitement, I wanted to hear more and more, the more detail the better.

My Dad asked everyone into the living room to continue the conversation. He added wood to the fire and sat in his chair that faced the brick fireplace. I sat on the floor in front of the fireplace with my heart pounding. My ears have never been so attentive. My Aunt and Mom could not have made it into the living room slower if they wanted to. I sat there waiting for them as my Dad slowly packed his pipe. Eventually my Aunt sat on the couch that was beside the small round wooden table that was beside my Dad's dark, worn, reddish brown, leather chair. My Mom followed with a tray of brownies and of course, chocolate chip cookies. Aside from the sounds of my Dad puffing on his pipe and my sisters playing behind the couch, the room was silent. A couple of barely audible creeks in the wooden floor beneath the worn carpet gave my Dad his cue to continue. He looked over to his sister who was looking over the drawings in the journal and reading here and there, "He really was a remarkable man," he said to no one in particular. My Aunt nodded her head in agreement. Almost at once everyone reached for the dessert tray that my sisters discovered moments earlier. For hours we sat there talking of Great Grandpa, his journal, Santa Claus, and how lucky we each are to have such a wonderful family. On that Christmas Eve Eve, in the comfort of our small living room, we celebrated.

June 5

Last night I said that I really should leave tomorrow. The Clauses said that I was welcome to stay as long as I wished, but I knew I had to leave. As bad as I wanted to stay I had to return home victorious and end all worrying about my well-being. Today being my last, it was full of preparation for the return voyage. I was given plenty of food by Mrs. Claus. The elves made me a wonderfully detailed and waterproof map along with a new compass. Then Santa and the elves worked together on the repairs done to my sled and gear. I spent the beginning of the day preparing my gear and letting the dogs know that we were leaving tomorrow morning. I realize how this must sound, but the reindeer and my dogs seem to have really become friends. In fact with the conditions that the dogs have become accustomed to I could see why they wouldn't want to leave. Of course if they don't leave with me than I guess I would have to wait for a flight home on Christmas Eve with Santa. Just kidding of course. On my many trips in between the house and the barn I saw several little, and I mean little, footprints. These little footprints in the snow were leading from about every building. I stopped the first time I noticed them and waited, hoping to see one. When I would return back outside there would be another trail of little footprints that weren't there before. It was both a wonderful and aggravating experience to see this. In the end however it was just plain wonderful, to see trails of little elf footprints leading through this North Pole village.

When I was alerted that it was lunchtime I had finished preparing my gear for the long trek home. As I sat there at the kitchen table enjoying another excellent lunch by Mrs. Claus I began to feel a little sad. I could tell that the Clauses were also sad. They had a lot of work to get back to and I had a family to get back to, and that was that. I had to be thankful for the time that I had with them. It would change my life forever. During lunch Santa told me that he had a surprise to show me before I left. After lunch we walked toward the workshop building. I remember that I wanted to believe that I would be allowed to see inside, and maybe even see an elf. As we approached the building Santa opened the large wooden door that had a million little stars carved in it. He motioned for me to enter. I hesitantly walked inside to see about ten stairs that led me down into a large room the size of a cornfield that ends only at the skyline. I stood there in an amazement that my body has never felt, an amazement that I never dreamed my mind and body were capable of feeling. I stood at the end of the largest workshop I have ever seen. There were hundreds of tables all surrounded by little workbenches. Each table also had a regular-sized workbench at the end, for Santa I assume. The floor and tables were covered in pieces of wire, plastic, metal and wood shavings. The tables were also full of little and normal size tools. In the middle of the room was a series of furnaces and conveyer belts. Standing there in total awe Santa came up to me and put his arm around my

shoulder, smiled, and shook his head in satisfaction. As he allowed me to stand there in silence I could make out the sound of saws and hammering coming from the floors below. I looked over to him and began to ask a *question. "They are fast at work, there are eight floors*

below this one, six of them larger than this one," he said.

I still stood there stunned and he continued, "I told

them that I wanted to show you this floor at least, so they

agreed to postpone work on the top floor for a short

time." Still just standing there I noticed what must have

been twenty elevators all along the walls of the

workshop. So many smells filled my nose, all together it

was the smell of hard work, a smell I will never forget. I

could have stood there for days but Santa gave me a pat

and we were off to the house. As he closed the door and

we made about five steps I could hear work begin on the

top floor. I could hear the saws start up and the

conveyer belts whirl into action. I wanted to run back

and open the door just to witness for a second the elves

at work, but I knew I should not, and could not.

As evening settled at Santa's village I wanted to ask

Santa a million more questions. Instead, I just enjoyed

their company over the last dinner I ever ate at the North

Pole. Before dinner Mrs. Claus asked me what I would

like, she said I could have anything my heart desired. I

began thinking but then stopped, I said to her that I

would rather enjoy whatever she and Santa would like. I
would like to enjoy my dinner with the Clauses eating
their favorite dish. She smiled and returned to the
kitchen. I spent those last hours looking around the
house. I looked at the maps in Santa's office. The maps
on the walls that had little notes and lines drawn all over
the place. Before I was ever told that I may make myself
at home, that I may look around as I choose, Santa also
said something interesting. He said, "...And George,
you will know where not to venture." As I looked at the
dozens of stacks of books that were about two and a half
feet by two feet I noticed the writing on the covers and
bindings, it read, "Good and Bad Boys and Girls."
Each of these books then had a number on them. I
slowly reached out to open the cover of one but stopped
myself; this was one example of where I knew I should
not venture.

The house once again began to fill with wonderful
smells. We sat again at the table that held a casserole of
potatoes, meat, carrots, and spices. The casserole was
covered in a layer of biscuits. I thought to myself how
neat it was that the Clauses enjoyed such a simple meal

as their favorite. They said that they enjoyed it so much because everything was combined in one spoonful. The Clauses live in a world of indescribable magic, yet they are such simple people. After dinner we sat in the den and just talked, we talked of nothing magical or having to do with the remarkable world in which they live, we just talked by the fireplace. We all retired to bed at the same time and I was asked when I planned on leaving. Santa said that he could get me up whenever I pleased. I asked him to get me up when he got up, he gave me a look and asked if I was sure, and I said yes. I did not care how early it was, I wanted to be awakened by Santa Claus on my last morning at the North Pole.

June 6

I and my dogs now lay in the tent that Santa and his little helpers built for me. This tent is remarkably warm and allows a little air to circulate. What wonderful craftsmen they are! This morning was sad and exciting. After a large breakfast Santa helped me pack my sled. I said my good-byes to the reindeer and was given yet another package of food by Mrs. Claus. As we said our long good-byes and gave our hugs I looked down at my compass because I wanted a picture of me with the dogs and the flag at exactly the North Pole. Santa took me to the actual North Pole and I found myself at the center of the village where a red and white striped pole stood about four feet tall. He put the compass on top of the pole and the needle pointed South, to the magnetic Pole. I knew that a picture of the North Pole village was not allowed so he offered to take me to the magnetic North Pole, South of the Village. Before the ride it was explained to me that the magnetic North Pole has moved as much as 12 degrees Southward in Santa's lifetime. It goes without saying that geography is one of Santa's hobbies, as well as celestial navigation. He attributed the movement of the Pole to the perpetual movement of the molten iron in the center of the earth's core. And there I stood at the magnetic North Pole with the American Flag just to my right and my sled and team behind me as I held out the compass with the needle spinning.

My gear, the dogs, and I were loaded in Santa's sleigh and were given a head start back home by Cupid, Blitzen, and Dasher. The sleigh moved across the frozen ground faster than anything I have traveled in before. Several hours passed and Santa asked if this spot were far enough, unsure as to how far we traveled in that time I thanked him for the head start. Before I left he told me that he would keep an eye on me to make sure that I made it back safely, which gave me all of the confidence in the world concerning my safety. I wanted to be sad as we rode off in different directions but strangely I was not. I did not want to leave, but I did. It all came together in me as something it was time to do. It was as simple as that. My dogs mushed like they were only a half- mile away from home, and I smiled the entire day. Writing about my day to day voyage back home seems trivial now. I just want to get there, and I will use the time it takes to get there to enjoy the memories that will never leave me.

June 7

Of course I am lonely, very lonely. I talk with my dogs, sing out loud, and think a lot. I marvel at the beauty that comes with white. The plain color that I see day and night. The port to Ellesmere Island will be a very welcomed sight. I am, however, well suited for the journey home. The dogs are in good spirits and I have a thousand wonderful memories to conjure up at any time I wish. One question that I did come up with today was what nationality Santa is? When I stayed with him I assumed he was American. He talked and acted like an American. Of course, it is known that he can speak every language in the world fluently. When I was in his library many of the books I picked up were written in different languages. Some of the letters he was writing on his desk were in German, Italian, and even Chinese. The conclusion that I came up with is that Santa is of no single nationality. He is half elf and lives at the North Pole. I guess that anyone, of any country, speaking any language, can meet Santa and assume that he is of their particular corner of the world. He is the most of everything that is wonderful, kind, magical, and good and he is limited only by belief.

That was just one of the questions that entertained my mind today in this world that contains only me and my dogs. I fall asleep finishing the drawings of the North Pole village.

June 8

I estimate that I am about fourteen days away from the port to Ellesmere Island, a sight that I think to myself is only a day away. The scrambling fury displayed by my dogs makes me think that they also believe that our destination lies just beyond our sight. They are showing an energetic and positive attitude. So far the weather, aside from the extreme cold and blistering winds, is excitingly bearable. I have yet to reach any stage of fatigue; I give myself about four to six more days of this until my body aches without reserve. I will no doubt return home too exhausted to jump directly into any talk concerning my great adventure.

June 12

The excitement of being only ten days from home is building fast. I am showing signs of great exhaustion. My new, well worn in gloves that were made for me by the Clauses are keeping my fingers from attaining even the slightest signs of frostbite. The socks that they gave me are working the same miracles for my feet. I stop several times a day to check on the sled and above all the condition of the dogs. They are extremely tough, after each stop they cannot wait to continue on, they bark and paw at the ground until I release the brake and the sled speeds off. These dogs really do have an instinctual passion for this.

Today the first excursion of the trek home found us. At around 2:00 in the afternoon I slowed the dogs to make out what my eyes could not at speed. As we approached the unusual look in the surface I noticed that the ice and snow melted enough to create a slowly flowing river about thirty feet wide. I had no choice but to stop the dogs and unhook them. I set up the tent and we climbed in to keep warm while I fed them and myself.

We just waited until this temporary river froze. At about 3:45 I awoke in the tent to find my dogs asleep. I slowly opened the tent in order to check on the condition of the river, and to my satisfaction it appeared refrozen. I quietly stepped out so as to not unnecessarily awaken the dogs. I thoroughly checked, and it was undoubtedly frozen. On my return to the tent I noticed little elf footprints in the snow right around the tent. I followed the prints all the way around the tent only to find them disappear as they ventured off. As I packed up the wind began to become fierce, beating us on all sides. We got moving and I sent the dogs across what used to be a river on account of their light weight. I then crossed pushing the sled. Although it was difficult to tell exactly where the former river began and ended due to the wind pushing snow all over the place, I guessed that I was about 3/4 of the way across it. I then heard a deep solid cracking sound. I slowly made it down to my belly and inched my way across, all the while my dogs barked as they waited on the land I could not wait to feel under my feet. The cracking sound continued but much more silently and slowly. I made it to the other side and stood there relieved for a minute or so. I stood there just looking at my sled that sat on the ice. I took the whip and small round of rope that I had tied to my jacket. I tied the two together and slowly made my way back to the sled on my stomach. When I reached the sled I let out a large breath of air and attempted to listen for any ice cracking. Then in a sudden thought of sense I decided not to wait for anything, I tied one end of the rope to the sled and I inched my way back to the dogs. I then slowly pulled the sled to me and took a short break in total satisfaction and luck. Within ten minutes we were on our way, praying for a total lack of obstacles. Again I lay in my tent finding it hard to keep my eyes open.

June 15

I apologize to the reader for skipping so many days in this diary of my expedition but you must understand how tired I am on some nights. Some nights, like tonight, I fall asleep thinking only of my return.

June 16

On this day pieces of home came to me. With only
seven days to the port to Ellesmere Island left I saw six
men carried by sled dogs coming on the horizon.
Excitement in me began to build and the dogs sensed it.
I could tell that they sensed it because they began to
build their own excitement and carried me across the
frozen ground faster. As I approached the group we
slowed until I recognized my fellow short-lived
explorers. Immediately I was happy to see them along
with the other four men who held their company. Then
for a second, and only a second, a feeling of
disappointment and anger filled my memories of them.
By the time we came to a stop and the dogs greeted each
other, I was overcome with the usual joy of seeing long
lost friends, or even people for that matter. We hugged,
and introduced, and slapped each other hard on the
backs.

Throughout their questions and explanations, I
remained quiet as to what happened concerning 'you-

know-who." They admired my new sled and gear and I simply told them it was a gift from the Eskimos. I was too tired to begin any stories that require such odd looks and explanations. We decided to camp right where we met. They brought food, whiskey and one man brought a harmonica. All combined it was one big welcoming party. Not a welcome home, but a welcome back to my society. We laughed and told stories. I was told that everyone was worried about me and that some of the papers considered me dead. The good news was that most of the papers, and more importantly my family, knew that I was still alive and that by this point I reached the North Pole.

June 19

The days are flying by now. We sled over the frozen tundra together with smiles on our faces and home on our minds. For me I return to the home that has occupied my thoughts ever since I left my front porch. For my old friends and the new ones, they are returning *home with a hero that they gladly found still alive. Four days left.*

June 22

Tonight we sleep comfortably at the port to Ellesmere Island. We arrived a whole day early and I am told that a boat will come at around 7:00 tomorrow morning. I can not wait until I can awaken and put on the only pair of clean clothes that I have left. I have been saving these clothes for the return. I now wonder if I will be able to sleep at all knowing that I will be on my way home tomorrow. Although my body aches from such a voyage and my mind wonders through the two realities that I now know exist, I still find myself awake with the simple excitement that comes with a return home. The hero's welcome that I yearned for when I set out on this adventure is now a small treat when compared with seeing my family and Virginia again. I figure that no matter how rich or poor one is, or where their home is, if there is one at all, there is a place whether physical or imagined, that makes a man at home. I explore not to

find myself or my home, I know where both are, instead I
explore to see what God did when I was not around.

And with that my Great Grandfather ended the
journal. Later we found 37 journals in the attic, they
were accounts of explorations from Asia to Ireland, from
Alaska to Chile. But none were as exciting as this one,
for obvious reasons. None of the others referred to little
green men or any other unusual events for that matter.
No, this journal was legitimate, it proved to us that Santa
Claus does in fact exist, and he lives at the North Pole.
Our attic also housed the sled that Santa made for my
Great Grandfather. My Great Grandfather was credited
with being the first to explore the North Pole in the
papers when he returned home. He did not sound the
alarm. Instead, his friends did. George Platt returned
home satisfied without the fanfare that comes with being
the first to explore the North Pole. Therefore, he
declined interviews and refused the proof that certain
geographic organizations asked for on his return. The
media quickly dismissed his exploration as being an
unsuccessful attempt. My Grandmother told me that his

friends and family begged him to show everyone the proof that he did in fact have. He refused, and in the journal were the pictures of him standing at the North Pole next to the Stars and Stripes.

My Great Grandfather's journal gave my family a special spirit of celebration on that Christmas of 1980. We all had a renewed belief in such things St. Nick. I am now a 29 year old, still living in the house that my Great Grandfather built, and I bring you George Platt's journal because every now and then we need to be reintroduced to that jolly old man.

#